TH

IN TH_ STONE

Written by

SP K-Mushambi

Illustrated by

Kudzai Ngundu & Andrew Mandaza

For my beautiful daughters Danai & Tayana

To Marley Anesu

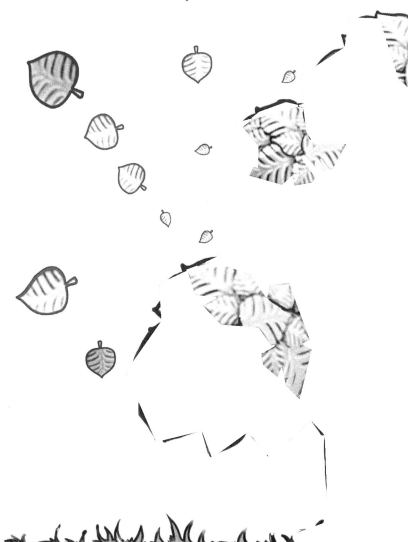

CONTENTS

CHAPTER 1

A STRANGE STARING CONTEST

It was certainly out of character and not like Shinga at all!

This went against everything, *everything* that *Baba* and *Amai* had taught him. Locking horns with the old man was not in the 'respect your elders' *tsika* lecture he constantly received. But if anyone was going to win a staring competition it was going to be him. Shinga's usually calm manner was rattled. His nostrils flared up like those of an angry bull; his hands clenched in fists at his sides and his feet were firmly planted to the ground in defiance. Nothing and no one would make Shinga back down until he got back what was his—his football.

Now if you knew Shinga you would know this behaviour was quite odd indeed. Yes, he could wear you down in an unnecessarily long debate just to prove his point. Yes, there was the fact that he liked to annoy his twin Naniso. In his defence he would say she was the annoying one. But one thing you could count on was that he was a cool guy. Most of the time, he was a calm, sensible and caring 10-year-old. That was, of course, until that afternoon. Something about the old man had totally ruffled Shinga's feathers.

"Can you give us back the football please?" Shinga asked the old man for a third time as he stood just a few metres in front of him. He suddenly realised that his tone was rude. *Amai would be so disappointed*, he thought to himself, but he kept his gaze and his distance.

Okay, let's rewind a bit. How did we get to this point? You see, Shinga had been kicking the ball around after school in the park with his friends

Sanjay and Mason. They had football trials for the county clubs coming up soon and were trying to get in as much practice as they could. Each of the boys had a good chance of being selected. But, Shinga had recently and oddly seemed a little less eager for the opportunity than the others. Coach had even called him out on his lack of focus. That had been an embarrassing moment. Shinga now wanted to prove Coach wrong. So, after school he decided to join Sanjay and Mason for some practice. During play, the ball had rolled to the great oak tree and was stopped at once by an imposing old man. Now on any other day, an old lady who Naniso fondly called *Gogo Zana* would have cheerily kicked the ball back to the boys. However, on this partly cloudy day, she had been replaced by a man who clearly had some crafty idea brewing in his head. Instead of returning the ball, he placed his right foot on it with no apparent intention of giving it back.

Sanjay had been the first to run up to ask for the football. His request had been ignored with a scoff. Mason had gone up next and he too had been snubbed. The boys had used all their politeness with smiles, 'excuse me-s' and 'please-s' but all they received was a cold and frosty glare. It was now Shinga's turn, and he was very upset by the way his friends had been unfairly treated.

The old man stared Shinga down with his small piercing eyes that sat in a thin, sunken face. His high cheekbones, wrinkly skin and emotionless expression gave him a haunted look. In fact, the wrinkles were like cruel slashes. However, despite his old age, he stood tall and proud and was elegantly dressed in a dark green West African-style tunic with gold trimmings and olive-green trousers. His shoes were pointy and so shiny that you could almost see your reflection in them.

It was at the sight of the clean shoes that Shinga lost the 'staring contest' and he dropped his gaze to stare at his own school shoes. They were new, but you would be forgiven for thinking otherwise judging by how muddy they were; not to mention the scratches from all the running and kicking. *Amai* had stopped complaining about him ruining good shoes all the time and had decided to buy him a cheap pair instead.

There was something reassuringly warm and familiar about the old man but at the same time his presence sent chills down Shinga's spine. Too upset to care, Shinga quickly shook off the fear. Just as he was about to ask for the ball again, the man kicked it to him. The ball rolled ever so slowly towards Shinga. The old man's eyes focused on the ball's path as though he was controlling its movement. It was only when Shinga stopped the ball with his foot did the man raise those piercing eyes and glare at him again.

"You bore me." The man finally spoke kissing his teeth in disgust. "And the old tree dare calls you *Muchengeti?*" He 'tsked' again and glanced at the oak tree as if waiting for it to respond. It was most peculiar to observe. After a moment he crouched to pick up a stone which he then tossed into the air a couple of times before examining it.

"This rough stone can easily be turned into something beautiful," he said in a gentle yet slightly terrifying voice.

"It's just a stone," Shinga blurted, rolling his eyes upwards.

"Pay attention!" the man commanded. "From the outside it looks like it's just a stone, but the right person will see that it's more than that." He paused than added in a whisper, "They may just see something special."

"But it is just a stone...," Shinga repeated himself slowly to make his point. He was in no mood for a lecture, *especially* a lecture from a stranger.

"But it's just a stone," the man mimicked Shinga and then asked, "Is it though?"

"What has that got to do with me?" Shinga asked dismissively.

"*Zvose!* — Everything!" The man yelled in frustration. "You are rough, negative and impatient. You lack commitment. You are not a team player, and you are becoming a selfish coward. Me. Me. Me. You carry on with this *Ini*-Me show and you will fail your next challenge," he spat with rage.

Shinga felt a hard lump form at the back of his throat. He was too choked with hurt to talk. No one had ever spoken to him like that before. Even though the old man's voice was quiet and soothing, the words were harsh and cruel. It was as if he had done it deliberately to make the words bearable for Shinga to hear. What was this man's problem?

Suddenly, Shinga saw a dark shadow fall across the man's face as a vulture swirled overhead. He logically explained it away by saying the sun was hiding behind the clouds.

"You. You... don't know me. I... I *am* a team player. Ask my friends," Shinga whined, visibly upset.

"No! *You* ask your friends." The old man's voice was now full of menace. "You are going to fail, and I will be right about you!" He shook his head, turned around and started to walk away.

"Wait! That's unfair! You just can't say horrid things and walk off!" Shinga protested but the man continued with a slow, confident pace. As he passed under the oak tree, he snapped off a twig from one of the branches. Shinga thought he saw a flicker of golden dust float into the air where the twig had broken off. In that instance, in his mind's eye, the oak tree magically changed to a majestic upside-down tree with a wise-looking face carved on its trunk. One of the branches bent downwards and sprinkled water that was nestled in its leaves onto a black flower growing from the ground below. The tree's face smiled and this somehow calmed Shinga. After blinking one-two-three times to clear his mind, he saw a squirrel scamper up the now familiar oak tree. Strange? *My mind is clearly playing tricks on me*, he thought.

"Hey? And what do you mean a tree called me *Muche... Muchengeti*?" he called to the old man who was by then almost at the park gate. A few fallen dry leaves danced around his feet as he walked out of the gate.

Then, he vanished!

The sun was now peering through the clouds again and Shinga's stomach was growling. Naniso would have a spare breakfast bar in her backpack and he was most certainly going to help himself to it. Just then Sanjay and Mason joined him, and with a broad smile on his face, Shinga picked up the football.

"Weird right?" Mason flicked his unruly blonde hair from his eyes.

"Very weird. Do you know that man? He really wanted to talk to you," Sanjay said, flashing the blue braces on his teeth.

"I don't know him at all," Shinga said quickly. He wanted to forget about what had happened.

"C'mon then, let's play. This time Shinga keep your head in the game and pass the ball," Sanjay said as he grabbed the football from Shinga and showed off with a stepover trick before running off to get started.

CHAPTER 2

NANISO'S CURIOSITY

In the park Naniso sat cross-legged on a bench under the great oak tree. This was her favourite spot. She'd had a terrific day at school and had earned herself a special silver badge which she could not wait to show her parents. It would most certainly guarantee her a treat. A trip to McDonalds was what she would suggest to them. However, that was going to have to come later as now she had to wait for her brother and his friends. Shinga's football trials were a *big* deal and Naniso wanted to show her support. After all, the twins had vowed to always have each other's back. It was a pact they liked to seal with a high five, interlocking their fingers and saying '*Pamwe*' in unison which meant 'together' in the

Shona language. Shinga had been there for her at her violin exam. He had sat patiently as she ran through her scales and set pieces. She had been awarded a distinction—and for sure Shinga's support had a lot to do with that.

Naniso was lost in her geography book and had not witnessed Shinga's tense encounter with the old man. The book had once belonged to *Amai*. It was tattered and flimsy. Naniso turned the pages carefully in case they fell apart at the seams. She liked this book because it represented everything that *Amai* was against.

"Don't write in books!" That is what *Amai* would always say but, in this book, there were hundreds of notes scribbled in the margins of every page.

"Use a bookmark and don't fold the page!" That was another of *Amai*'s rules, but this book had many dog-eared pages and food stains. Eww!

Naniso had been reading about The Great Dyke which sounded like the biggest of treasure chests ever. It had gold, silver, emeralds, platinum and plenty of other minerals she had never heard of. Surely there was nothing richer. She could not wait to boast about all this knowledge of their country, Zimbabwe.

"What are you reading?" Shinga and his ball caught her by surprise as it almost hit her in the face.

"Stop bothering me. Go and practise with your friends." Naniso's hand shooed him away as if he were a pesky fly.

"I'm a football natural and have done enough for today," Shinga retorted and flashed her a big smile.

"I'm discombobulated. I thought you needed to put in the practice. Your coach told you to because you were off your game."

Shinga gazed at her over his glasses. Naniso was at it again. She had found a new big word and was using it wherever she could. Yup — 'discombobulated' was her new big word.

"No need to be confused, Sis. Besides, my friends have gone home." He sat next to her

peering into her book and adjusted his dusty, finger-smudged glasses.

"Ah The Great Dyke again?" Shinga exclaimed. He admired how his sister was like a sponge when it came to learning about their native country. For weeks now she had gone on and on about how rich it was with its different minerals and stones.

"Ahhhhhh stick your nose out of my book Shinga!" Naniso slammed it shut.

"Okay," Shinga mumbled, digging through his sister's bag for a snack.

"Stay out of my stuff!" Naniso snapped as she grabbed her bag from her twin. "What do you want anyway?" she demanded.

"A satisfying breakfast bar?" Shinga gave her a pleading smile.

"I should have guessed." She was not best pleased about being disturbed while reading.

"So, are you going to share or what?" Shinga ignored Naniso's grimace.

"Take it," she sighed, not wanting to get into an unnecessary squabble. *I'm having a good day*, she reminded herself.

"Do you know what *Muche... Muchengeti* means?" Shinga asked, unwrapping the cereal bar noisily.

"Yes, it's a Shona word. Where did you hear it?" Naniso's eyes lit up. She was all ears now.

"An old man called me that a little while ago."

"And you let him go?!" Naniso shouted excitedly. She instantly sprang to her feet and scanned the playground. Perhaps the old man was still there.

"You don't have to shout. Do you know him?" Shinga asked.

"I'm just curious that's all."

"Yeah, I can see that. Stop looking for him. He's long gone. Why are you so excited about that word? What are you hiding?"

"Nothing." Naniso looked disappointed.

"Sounds like something to me." Shinga was now curious.

"Alright. Someone also called me that once. You probably won't believe me. I mean you may think I am speaking rubbish but remember *Gogo* Zana? The old lady who came to the park?"

24

Naniso spoke so quickly and animatedly and excitedly that she did not give her twin a chance to respond. "I've not seen her since then. I think it was her... or maybe it was a chameleon. Rwaivhi the chameleon."

"What? A chameleon?" Shinga was trying to make sense of his sister's mutterings.

"Yeah, I know it sounds weird. It may have been a dream. Remember when we came to the park when I was nervous about playing the *mbira* at school for parent's assembly? Well, I had this weird experience. I was sitting right under this tree. Shinga, I felt like I was flying like a bird and next thing I was talking to animals and could really play the *mbira*. It was amazing. Someone called me *Muchengeti*, which means a guardian by the way. I was a guardian of the lost treasure. It was Rwaivhi, the chameleon who said it. A very cagey character at that too as she went on about how I had to 'learn these things on my own.' Please don't laugh at me or say I've gone crazy." Naniso covered her face with her hands in shame. She had said too much.

"I believe you," Shinga said, much to Naniso's surprise.

"You do? You are not discombobulated?" She was relieved.

"Are you sure you are using that word correctly? Okay, we'll figure this out together."

"*Pamwe*," Naniso added.

"Honestly, if I'd not met that man today, I would have said you were daydreaming too much." Shinga paused in thought as he twirled his football on his index finger.

"Tell me about this man?" Naniso asked.

"He was standing right under this tree but on the other side and refused to give us back our ball. Are you sure you didn't see him?"

"What did he say?"

"What I've already told you. He mentioned an old tree and said that word *Muche... Muchen...*"

"*Muchengeti*. It means guardian. Keep up. What else?"

"That's it," Shinga lied. He was not going to tell his sister that the old man had told him that he wasn't a team player and that he was also selfish.

As far as he was concerned, he was none of those things. Everyone liked him.

"What do we do?" he asked, hoping to steer Naniso away from her interrogation.

Naniso placed *Amai*'s book in her backpack whilst in deep thought. "Let's talk about it later. We must find out who this man is. If only we could find *Gogo* Zana."

"That little old lady who sometimes sits here? What would she know?" Shinga furrowed his eyebrows in confusion.

"Trust me, she knows," Naniso uttered with certainty.

CHAPTER 3

JEWELLED CARPET OF STONE

That night, lying in bed, Shinga ran through the day's events. He thought of the incident with the old man. It had been a little terrifying. He so wished he had said something clever back at him. Instead, he had been mocked and called names.

"No commitment. Not a team player. Negative. Coward!" The elderly man had practically jeered at him. Those were harsh words to say to someone, especially a child.

Shinga stared at the new and empty bed on the opposite end of the room. The wall next to the bed was now clear of his football and basketball posters. Cousin Ruzivo would be arriving tomorrow. He turned to face the ceiling and let out a huge sigh of disappointment. His family's routine was about to be disrupted. Things were going to change. But not being one to deny himself sleep, he was soon in dreamland.

Shinga dreamt that he was standing under an upside-down tree, a baobab tree to be specific. Words floated in his dream:

*Known as the **tree of life**, source of **water** and **shelter***

Superfood

*Can live for **over 3000 years***

The tree had a warm and wise face. It was old, ancient even, massively wide and with a bark that had ever-changing dancing patterns. Beneath the tree proudly grew a beautiful flower with black, velvety petals. The setting was a savannah landscape where the tranquil atmosphere was broken by the whisper of the gentle breeze. A boy, just a few years younger than Shinga, waved at him vigorously. Without thinking, Shinga waved back. The boy's hair was styled in a cool ruffled afro, and he wore blue shorts and a golden-orange

t-shirt with an embroidered picture of the upside-down tree. On his right arm, like an accessory, comfortably sat a chameleon.

The ground was a jewelled carpet of different minerals and stones that stretched to the distant mountains. This must have been The Great Dyke that Naniso was always on about. The boy closed his eyes, raised his arm with palm facing down and the stones floated up and circled him. It was a spectacular sight and Shinga was too scared to blink just in case he missed something or worse, woke up. The boy grabbed a stone and reached out to give it to Shinga.

"*Mangwanani*—Good morning. Welcome to Tirivhu, *Muchengeti*" the boy said. "We need your help. You will need this." Shinga accepted the stone without hesitation. His dream continued with Naniso playfully trying to catch a green emerald. He leapt to catch a gemstone too but before he could totally immerse himself into the mystical setting, the upside-down tree, the boy, chameleon, Naniso and the mineral carpet suddenly vanished.

Shinga woke up with a start to the sound of a fading enchanting melody. His right fist was clasped tightly. He slowly peeled away his fingers hoping to see the stone the little boy had given him. There was nothing. It had just been a dream...

Chapter 4

Tarirai Is Chosen

Faraway and yet ever so near, in the enchanted land of Tirivhu, Nhema paced up and down. All was still in nervous anticipation... all except the crunch of the dead leaves he trampled on. Back and forth he paced. He had been summoned!

"Aaaaaaargh!" he groaned, as if in great pain. Old Bao, the baobab tree and Zana, his sister wanted to talk. That could only mean one thing. They had found out he had spoken to the boy and were not pleased. Nhema let out an evil laugh so loud it scared the animals that were watching him nearby. Only a vulture perched on a branch of a msasa tree was unmoved by his presence.

Nhema slowly stroked his goatee beard. Pacing back and forth, he pondered over how he would wriggle himself out of being scolded by the old tree and his sister. He could say it wasn't him. But the old tree seemed to know everything. He could ignore the summons and not go. That was not an option at all though; you see, in the land of Tirivhu, if an elder called for your presence, you had to obey. Well, Old Bao had summoned him and there was no ignoring the elder. Nhema stopped pacing, straightened his back, and absent-mindedly ran his fingers over his deep wrinkles. He quickly gathered himself into a dusty whirlwind and set off to face his imagined ruin.

"*Masikati*—good afternoon," Nhema said as he approached Zana who was sipping her tea from a colourful, dainty cup. "Ah wonderful. A cup of tea. *Mazvita*—thank you."

Zana coughed violently as Nhema shape-shifted from a dusty whirlwind to a chameleon. He perched on Zana's tablecloth. Without warning, he changed his mind and swiftly transformed into his human form. His sudden movements knocked his sister off her chair and spilled some of her tea.

"Nhema, *gara pasi*—sit down." Zana sucked air through her teeth while cleaning the mess he had made.

"*Rina manyanga hariputirwe*—you cannot hide a horned animal by wrapping it," Bao added, ignoring the ruckus that Nhema was causing. The birds nested on his colourful branches tweeted in agreement.

"Bao, you must stop with your *tsumo* starters. No one pays attention. Must you start every conversation with a proverb?" Nhema scoffed. The majestic tree remained silent.

"Bao is right. That which has horns cannot be hidden," Zana broke the tension. "Remember at the Tirivhu Festival when sable antelope tried to fool everyone that he had no horns by tying a *dhuku*—headwrap—over them? He wanted to be part of the zebra parade." Zana chuckled at the memory.

"Hehe, I remember. That never worked, eh. No amount of cloth could hide those horns.

He looked ridiculous," Nhema replied. Both he and Zana giggled hysterically until their sides hurt.

"You both know the proverb means all wrongdoing will always come to light. When you two are done laughing there is a serious matter we need to discuss." Bao spoke sternly.

Nhema and Zana sheepishly quietened down and sat still. They both stared at the ground because they knew that if they looked at each other, they would start laughing all over again.

"You need to lighten up Old Man. I know why I'm here," Nhema bragged.

"Explain yourself Nhema. Your deceitful and dangerous actions do not go unnoticed. You could get Shinga into trouble by making him doubt himself," Bao said firmly.

Instantly Nhema's playful manner became dark and menacing. The clouds above turned grey. A vulture flew round and round in circles above them. Zana quickly grabbed her walking stick which gave off tiny golden sparks as it tapped the ground.

"I've told you time and time again, that boy is not worthy of the treasure. Whatever heroic plan you have for him, he will fail. I will prove to you that he does not deserve it. They all don't deserve it. C'mon, just let me have a little fun."

"You want to have fun? Do you even remember how?" Zana mocked her brother. Ignoring her, Nhema continued.

"They do not care about who they are. Always after what someone else has. They are quick to dismiss anything that's not shiny. They do not deserve the true treasures of this world. Scattered families! Killing the spirit of *ubuntu*!" He paused to take a heavy breath. "I will not be a guardian of these people's heritage treasure any longer. I wear the scarred wrinkles as a token of their ungratefulness. This belongs to those in Tirivhu. This now all belongs to us...!" By then he was shouting, and Zana cut him off.

"*Iwe* Nhema! Stop with your nonsense. Our duty is to help them know their truth and take pride in their heritage."

"C'mon! You must be joking. It is clear to me that these people have forgotten who they are. They don't want to know and they don't want the treasure. They would rather wait to moan when it's gone. Fools!" Nhema sprayed spittle as he spoke.

"We must help them. Our duty is to keep the flame alive. They are heirs of Tirivhu too," Zana calmly reminded him.

"No!" Nhema cried. "Look at me! This is what you get for helping...," pointing in despair at his wrinkled face before clasping his head in his hands.

The three were silent for a moment. Bao and Zana felt Nhema's pain. It certainly did not help that Shinga looked like the boy from Nhema's past. Zana sat down at the table and took a sip of the rest of her now cold tea. Nhema knelt next to a black flower growing between Bao's roots and clasped it as if to uproot it. Bao and Zana pretended not to notice.

"If Shinga can keep the flame burning, I may step aside. If he fails, then he cannot be *Muchengeti.*

The treasure stays in Tirivhu." Nhema spoke with a finality.

"*Siya* Shinga. Leave him alone," Zana protested.

"Like I said...," Nhema started again, but was interrupted.

"And I say you leave Shinga alone. Listen to your sister," Bao said impatiently as he shook his branches in disapproval of Nhema's stubbornness.

Zana nodded her head in agreement with Bao. This surely meant she would be picked to take up the role of being the twins' only guardian on this part of their journey to becoming *Vachengeti*. With Nhema's terrible attitude and disobedience there was no way Bao would pick him over her. Surely not. Zana sat tall, waiting for Bao's instruction.

"Tarirai will be their guardian." With that order, Bao shattered Zana's hopes.

"Tarirai? He is but a child. Is this a joke?" Nhema laughed in disbelief.

"Tarirai?" Zana echoed quietly.

"*Hongu* — Yes, Tarirai." Bao noticed that Nhema and Zana were about to argue why it should be one of them.

"*Zvakwana*—That is all for now," the ancient tree said. He closed his eyes as if in meditation, a sure sign that the matter was not up for debate. Zana poured herself another cup of tea and considered Bao's decision. It felt unfair, even silly, but it was wise.

Zana and Nhema looked at each other suspiciously. They knew that neither of them would stay away from whatever adventure Tarirai had with the twins. Tarirai was just a young guardian in training. A little boy. While Zana believed that she could gently help him guide the twins, Nhema saw an opportunity to cause havoc and prove Shinga's weakness. He would then be a step closer to keeping the heritage treasure in Tirivhu.

"I guess this is where we go our separate ways for now, *hanzvadzi*—my dear sister," Nhema said mischievously.

They both sat in silence under the baobab tree, sipping tea.

CHAPTER 5

EVERYTHING'S ABOUT RUZIVO

Back in England, unaware of the plans taking shape in the mystical land of Tirivhu, the twins arrived home from another day at school. One was anxious and the other excited. Cousin Ruzivo was coming to stay. Soon *Baba* would be home from the airport with him. The unmistakeable aroma of wood floor polish and roasting chicken greeted Naniso and Shinga as they walked through the front door and dropped their bags in the hallway. *Amai* would no doubt tell them off for not putting things where they belonged. She was in the kitchen icing a red velvet cake with delicious cream cheese frosting.

"Wow! Are the Royals coming for dinner?" Naniso teased her mother as she gazed at a buffet all laid out on the kitchen table. "Do you think they have eaten sadza before?"

There was a black pot on the stove with *sadza* ferociously bubbling inside.

"They may have," *Amai* responded warmly and greeted the twins with a hug. "Now go and wash your hands," she instructed firmly.

Amai had surely prepared a banquet with all sorts. There was rice, beef stew, spiced roasted chicken, *dauphinoise* potatoes, *muriwo*—fresh greens, some plantain, coleslaw and even mac 'n' cheese. Shinga reached out to pick up a piece of chicken and quick as a flash, *Amai* gently slapped his hand away.

"Not now Shinga," she scolded.

"I'm not sure what all the fuss is about. This food could feed an army. Who cares if Ruzivo is coming to stay?" Shinga grumbled. He was surprised at how irritable his voice sounded. Worse, he could feel *Amai*'s gaze burn through him like a laser. Naniso gave him a nudge for speaking out of turn.

"*Mukoma!*" *Amai* burst out. She narrowed her eyes and looked at both Naniso and Shinga with a no-nonsense expression.

"Ruzivo is your big brother. That means he is *Mukoma* Ruzivo to you. *Mukoma*, do you hear?"

The twins nodded and knew better than to argue with their mother, especially when she spoke in that tone. Addressing Ruzivo with this title seemed very important to her. They were used to this kind of conversation especially if there were relatives around. They had such a large, extended family and could not keep track of who was who, how to address them or why to address them. In Shinga's opinion all the protocol was unnecessary. Ruzivo was their cousin and that was that. Too much attention had been given to his arrival so far, and to make matters worse, he, Shinga, had to share his bedroom with him. *Baba* had put up that new bed from Ikea. He could have helped but he preferred to sulk and play a video game instead. All the bed did was take up the space he used for his stuff.

Ruzivo was Naniso and Shinga's first cousin on their father's side of the family. His father was Baba's older brother meaning that he was *Babamukuru* — 'big father'. Apparently in the Shona language there was no such thing as uncle. However, to call Ruzivo just a cousin would be an insult and make their relationship distant. Ruzivo was their brother. His father was also their father and received the same status and respect as they would give *Baba*. This, Naniso and Shinga had been told, ensured loyalty and strength within the family. However, Ruzivo's arrival made Shinga uncomfortable, yet it filled Naniso with joy.

"Aww he looks just like you Shinga," Naniso gasped.

Ruzivo stood tall in the hallway. He was about five foot ten with a neat, short afro. His wide, warm smile showed that he was pleased to see his young 'siblings' who were now a lot taller than when he had last seen them. Naniso got a hug and a reluctant Shinga got a brotherly pat on the shoulder. Shinga's unusually bad mood had not disappeared. *This was no way to welcome a guest*

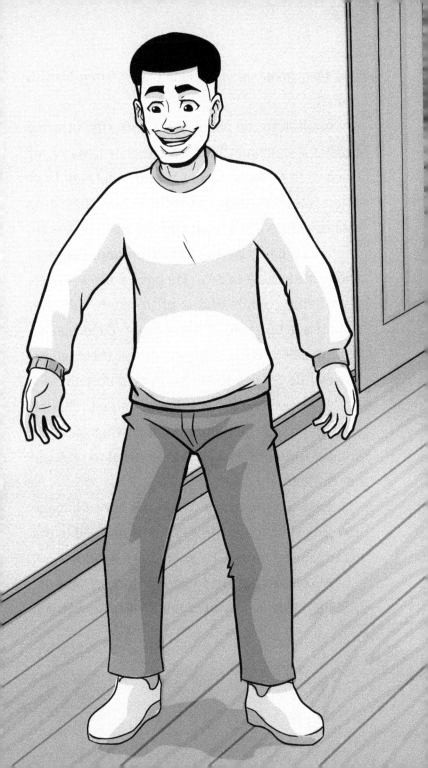

into their home. Shinga knew to act better, Naniso thought.

Amai fluttered about like a butterfly, offering Ruzivo a welcome drink of either tea, water, or Coca-Cola (which usually meant whatever fizzy drink was available). The twins helped *Baba* drag his heavy bags up the stairs into Shinga's bedroom.

"You'll enjoy having Ruzivo around. I bet you will learn a thing or two. He passed his A' Levels with flying colours and is off to study robotics. Robotics I tell you. What a guy!" *Baba* gushed then headed back downstairs to their guest. Meanwhile, Shinga rolled his eyes in despair.

"I know you're not happy about sharing your room, but he'll only be here when he is on holiday from university," Naniso tried to reassure her brother.

"Easy for you to say. You don't have someone invading your space. Where am I supposed to put my organised mess?" He sulked like a toddler.

"*Mukoma* is not just someone Shinga. Come on. Don't let *Amai* hear you say that," Naniso warned.

"Whatever! Leave me alone."

"This might not be so bad. *Mukoma* Ruzivo seems nice. Give him a chance." With that Naniso left her brother to his sulking.

"Yeah, whatever," he huffed, straightened his glasses then waited a few minutes before going to join the family.

There was a lot of noisy laughter and excited chatter coming from the living room as Shinga walked down the stairs. He stopped to sit on the creaky 11th step. That step, along with the ninth, always creaked even after *Baba* and a handyman had 'fixed' it. A chill ran up his spine as he felt a sudden breeze.

"I suppose I could try and be nice," Shinga said to himself without much faith. Although he wanted to be, he remained angry about having to share his room. As far as he was concerned, his family had betrayed him and his privacy.

He just could not see what good would come out of having him around. *Amai* would not even let him, her favourite boy, sneak a piece of chicken into his mouth. She would normally have turned a blind eye. Shinga sighed in frustration. For weeks now, everything had been about Ruzivo. Ruzivo this and Ruzivo that and oh you are to address him as *Mukoma*. A title — as if he were someone special!

Shinga, the calm and reasonable twin, was truly bothered.

CHAPTER 6

THE GIFTS

Shinga unwillingly dragged himself from the stairs and joined the family in the living room. *Baba* and *Amai* took the lead asking after each family member back in Zim. *This will take a while*, Shinga thought to himself. There was a lot of clapping with the familiar greeting, "*Makadi, makadi?* — How are you?"

"*Makadi Mukoma,*" Naniso asked Ruzivo enthusiastically. You could count on Naniso to play ball.

Ruzivo responded that he was well and that he was proud of Naniso's Shona. Shinga however was tongue-tied. Naniso willed her brother to just say the one word and help the family move past the awkwardness. This was the 'Tete-gate' incident all over again; the time when Shinga did not greet Tete as was expected in their Shona language and culture. How was it he could not say those three simple syllables, *Ma-ka-di*?

He pretended not to notice *Amai* cast him a disappointed look. Shinga continued to sit in the armchair staring at the blank TV screen in front of him. He could tell his mother was urging him on by occasionally bopping her head in his direction. He was not going to say it and he was certainly not going to clap while saying it. It always came out wrong with his British accent, and on top of that, it also felt weird. Shinga knew his mother would not dismiss him until he had said the greeting and just could not understand what the fuss was about. Ruzivo, who had been pretending not to notice the silent battle between mother and son, broke the tension and asked,

"How are you Shinga, *munin'ina*—young brother?"

"I'm fine," Shinga blurted out too quickly.

"I'm happy that I get this chance to spend time with you all. I heard you have soccer—

I mean football trials soon. I can't wait to see you play. I love football and I've missed it since my accident. Well enough of that, I have gifts from *Sekuru* and *Ambuya*," Ruzivo announced as he rummaged through the bag at his feet.

Out came a bundle wrapped in a blanket, newspaper and mounds of bubble wrap that their grandparents had sent. Once he had finally unwrapped it all, Ruzivo pulled out a tall, beautiful *ukama* sculpture, depicting a family embraced in a dance. It was at least the same height as the coffee table. Though he presented it as a gift for the family, really it was for *Amai*. This would no doubt become one of her prized possessions. The sculpture was hand-carved from a greenish-black natural serpentine stone and was polished to a bright shine.

Ruzivo then unwrapped some stones and gave one to Shinga and another to Naniso. Each stone was the shape of an egg, felt very smooth and had the same bright shine as the sculpture. Naniso was clearly delighted with her gift. *Baba* was overcome with emotion; this was a tradition

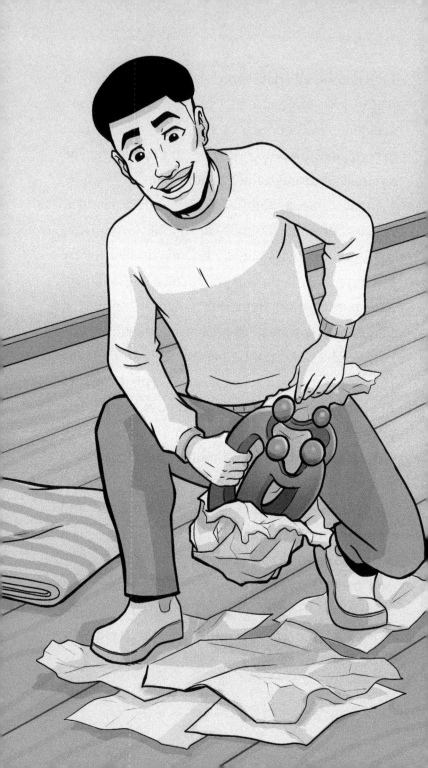

that *Sekuru* — grandfather to the twins had started and was passing on to them. It dawned on him that each member of *Sekuru*'s family was given a polished stone whenever *Sekuru* believed it was the right time. *Baba* had been gifted his when he was about the same age as Shinga. *Amai* received hers when she got married during the traditional *roora* — wedding ceremony. Ruzivo said he had a similar stone to Shinga's but had forgotten to pack it for his trip. He had carried it almost everywhere and felt a little lost without it. Not wanting to dwell too long on that he explained the significance of the stones to the twins. Shinga was not impressed, in fact he was willing to give up his stone to Ruzivo if that simple rock meant so much to him. His feet kept rubbing each other impatiently as if he needed the loo. As far as Shinga was concerned, while the stones were a cool gesture, he did not need Ruzivo to tell him about them. There was 'Naniso and The Great Dyke' or Google for that.

Unlike Shinga, the rest of his family were spellbound as they hung on to Ruzivo's every word. Shinga's tummy rumbled. He was hungry. It helped to think there was a feast waiting to be devoured.

"Your stone, Naniso, is the soapstone. Famous for..."

"...The stone sculpted birds found at the Great Zimbabwe ruins. Six of them found in the Eastern Enclosure. That is where royalty lived. The birds..."

"Naniso?" *Amai* chided her daughter for the unrestrained excitement. Addressing Ruzivo she added, "You must pardon h*anzvadzi yako*—your sister—she has been reading about The Great Dyke and the Great Zimbabwe Ruins."

"The House of Stone. Ah! Who then do you believe built Great Zimbabwe Naniso?" Ruzivo quizzed.

"The local Shona people, obviously. Who else?" Shinga abruptly answered.

"You're right, but did you know there had been many disagreements over that for years?

Most people couldn't believe that the local people could have built something so magnificent. Some even said it was built by the Queen of Sheba."

"What?!" The twins said at once, astonished, and disappointed by this revelation.

"It was obviously the local people," Shinga repeated, throwing his hands in the air. Ruzivo nodded and moved on to explaining the gifted stones.

"Shinga *munin'ina,* your stone is the serpentine. These come in a wonderful variety of colours. The colour *Sekuru* gave you is the same as mine because we are brothers," Ruzivo proudly mentioned.

Naniso's heart shrank as she noticed Shinga's mouth turn into a slight grimace. *What was wrong with him?*

"Thank you *Mukoma,*" Naniso spoke for them both.

"I'm hungry," Shinga announced loudly. He knew this would get *Amai*'s attention as their guest had not eaten yet.

Phew, Naniso thought to herself, *maybe food would cheer him up. Amai* quickly guided them to the dining table. After grace and thanksgiving prayers, everyone tucked into the delicious food. Within minutes, Shinga's growling stomach was finally satisfied. His mood was a little brighter.

CHAPTER 7

BEDTIME STORIES

Ruzivo settled well in his new home. He gave Naniso *mbira* lessons as he had learnt to play it at school and was brilliant at it. Naniso was delighted. He also taught his siblings some folk songs and stories he had heard from *Sekuru, Ambuya* and other elders in the family. No one could deny that he was a great teacher because soon Naniso was singing along to '*Kachembere kegudo'*, a folk song about an old baboon and her eight children. Together Naniso and Ruzivo remixed the song to a dancehall beat and it sounded amazing. However, no matter how many times they asked Shinga to join in, he always had an excuse. Most of his excuses were terrible like 'having to clean his room' (who was he kidding, of course he didn't). One evening, even *Baba* and *Amai* joined to dance to the Naniso & Ruzivo music production. Everyone had so much fun. Except Shinga. Secretly, he wished he had joined in, but he just could not bring himself to. He was indeed ruffled.

When it came to the school run and helping the twins with their school projects, Ruzivo was a star. It was super cool that he could drive too. Soon the twins learnt to ignore his constant complaints about the many roundabouts. That was mainly because he almost always treated them to ice-cream whenever he picked them up from school. Ruzivo had fast become a star volunteer at the afterschool club, Startbots, which he always insisted on referring to by its full name—Science, Technology, Art and Robots. He was polite and friendly with the parents at the school gate too—there Naniso beamed with pride standing next to him whilst Shinga brewed with resentment.

"I don't trust him," Shinga said to his friend Sanjay at football practice one afternoon a few weeks after Ruzivo had arrived. Ruzivo was cheering the team by the sidelines. He had a few weeks before university started and wanted to support Shinga at practice and matches.

"Why would you say that? He's family, right? I would be happy to have a big brother supporting my team. He's cool. It's a shame about his accident because I'm sure he could teach us a thing or two."

Shinga could not believe what Sanjay had said. Ruzivo had his friends under his spell too. That was enough. Who did he think he was? Ruzivo was in his space, and Shinga had to put an end to it.

It certainly did not help matters that Ruzivo and Shinga shared a bedroom. An invisible boundary divided the room in half. On one side was Shinga's organised mess. On the other, nothing was out of place except a book that was left carelessly on Ruzivo's bed. It was truly a case of complete opposites.

At night, when Shinga was trying to go to sleep or rather pretend to sleep, Ruzivo would just start telling him a story. Shinga listened half-heartedly. He could not believe that Ruzivo thought he was a toddler who needed bedtime stories. The stories were of imaginary adventures Ruzivo had made up when he was a little boy. They involved some superhero type who guided, protected and warned his people from The Lie. The hero's name was strange, something like '...*noparira*.' In the stories there was always a quest to find a flame and keep it alive. Shinga had never met anyone with quite an imagination like his cousin—except for Naniso. When he spoke about the 'superhero', Ruzivo's voice was always animated. He gave each character a different voice which brought the characters to life. For weeks, Ruzivo's adventures took them up a lit mountain trail, through dark caves, making a pact with a hare, or was it a baboon, and eating the most delicious mangos.

One night, Ruzivo simply said goodnight and went on to read a book. The superhero was gone, and the stories stopped. Shinga wished he had paid more attention. He had quietly started to enjoy this time of the day and was surprised that he missed the sound of Ruzivo's tales.

"What do you think happened to your superhero? Did he ever come back?" Shinga asked.

"I grew up and stopped making up stories," Ruzivo said. "But I remember sometime after I stopped, Sekuru gave me my stone. He told me the stone had a secret," he chuckled. "It really was just a smooth stone, but what made it extraordinary was that he had carved it himself. I sort of feel lost without it... strange." He went back to reading his book.

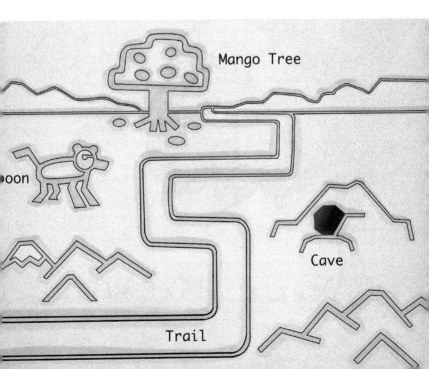

CHAPTER 8

SHINGA'S WAY

"You want me to what!?" Naniso could not believe what she was hearing.

"Don't shout. You want everyone to hear you?" Shinga tried to silence his twin.

"Well, if you don't want *Baba* and *Amai* to hear, then you know this is wrong," she hissed.

Football trials were coming up and Shinga did not want Ruzivo to come and watch. *Baba* had insisted that family needed to support each other. Shinga's newly crafted plan was for Ruzivo's support to be elsewhere — with Naniso. She would persuade him to take her to her piano lesson which was on the same day. *Amai* would come to the football trials instead. Naniso could, Shinga suggested, pretend to be sick after the lesson. Ruzivo would have no choice but to take her home. That way he would be nowhere near the football trials.

"I will owe you big time Sis," Shinga pleaded with puppy dog eyes.

"No. I won't do it. Besides, I like Ruzivo. You should be happy that he wants to come and see you play. He's been your biggest fan. Did you even notice that he makes sure your football kit is ready and that you have enough snacks and water in your bag? He even cleans your muddy football boots. Now, don't tell me you think a football fairy has been doing that for you? If you gave him a chance, he could give you a few tips."

"Why does everyone keep saying that? It's because of him that I am not doing so well with my football training."

"That's silly and you know it!" Naniso placed her hands on her hips.

"So, you are not going to help me? I help you all the time Naniso. If you don't want to, I will find my own way." He looked into the distance and stuffed his hands into his pockets.

Shinga's way did not work.

That afternoon he had decided to speak up. He had gathered all his courage, stood tall with chest pumped out and stared *Baba* in the eye. He told him that he did not want Ruzivo to come to his trials. *Baba* had not given him a moment to explain but instead insisted that Ruzivo joined them. That was that and he went on to repeat what he had said a million times since Ruzivo had arrived.

"You can learn a thing or two from your *Mukoma*. He can help you."

Deafened with anger and blinded with frustration, Shinga raised his voice and declared it was his life and his decision to make. The uproar had *Amai*, Naniso and Ruzivo appear in the hallway in time to witness Shinga stomp away in rage and kick the console table fiercely. To everyone's horror *Amai*'s prized *ukama* stone sculpture came crashing down on the wooden floor. Four heads became three. The detached head rolled and landed in front of their mother's feet.

Amai's hands flew to her hips. She was not at all pleased. Naniso, who always had something to say, was left dumbstruck. Her mouth flew wide open in disbelief. Something was clearly wrong with her brother. He was normally the caring, cautious and considerate one. There was an eerie silence until *Baba* bellowed in his baritone voice that Shinga was a disrespectful and selfish child. He repeated how disappointed he was that his own children, his flesh and blood, did not value the importance of family. Blaming the behavior on too much time spent on video games and on devices *Baba* unplugged the gaming console and confiscated the twins' phones, hiding them in an unknown place.

Shinga stormed to his bedroom muttering how unfair it all was. Naniso's protests fell on *Baba's* deaf ears. Instead, she helped *Amai* gather the broken stone pieces.

A little while later Naniso stood by Shinga's bedroom door. She wondered how long her twin brother would continue to ignore her knocking. All she wanted was to be a peacemaker.

"Shinga." Naniso tried to engage as she slowly crept into the bedroom. There was no response, just the sound of a tennis ball being thrown against the ceiling. Shinga lay on his bed sullen and focused on making as loud a noise as he could with that ball.

"Shinga..."

"Leave me alone Naniso," he snapped back. He scratched his forehead, a habit of his when he was a bag of nerves. Glasses falling off his face, he abruptly turned to his sister and aimed the ball at her. *What did she want*? he asked himself.

Naniso stood her ground. She held the now three-headed family of four.

"I didn't mean to break it," Shinga explained in defense.

"I know you didn't. Help me fix it. You know how valuable these sculptures are to *Amai*. Especially this one," Naniso reminded him.

Of course, Shinga knew that the stone sculptures were special to his mother. Every time they went to Zim, she went to the market to buy one to add to her collection.

As if reading her brother's mind, Naniso sat on the edge of his bed and said, "Remember, when *Amai* bought that hippo sculpture after our boat trip along the Zambezi River in Victoria Falls? It weighed over 20 kilos!"

"I'm surprised it made the long flight to England without a scratch," Ruzivo said, leaning against the doorway holding a football. "C'mon you two let's get some fresh air and maybe ice-cream too," he added, flashing a reassuring smile.

Ice-cream! The twins did not need to be asked twice.

CHAPTER 9

THE LADY ELDER

Naniso, Shinga & Ruzivo sat on the park bench quietly enjoying their ice-cream cones. Shinga and Ruzivo had chosen vanilla while Naniso opted for chocolate. There was a gentle breeze and dusk was drawing near. You could hear the evening birdsong.

Shinga recalled the day's events as he enjoyed his treat. A familiar yet weird feeling overcame him. Mystic music enveloped him as he felt himself floating. No, he was flying around the great oak tree and through its trunk! Then, he found himself standing next to Naniso in the middle of an enchanting landscape. The savannah sun was starting to set behind the distant mountain range. A giraffe was eating leaves from the tall branches of a nearby tree. A boy, the boy he had dreamt about the day Ruzivo arrived, was playing *mbira*. On his shoulder was a chameleon. Yes, it was him alright, with the same afro and a missing tooth that Shinga noticed today. The boy did not appear to notice them.

"I know that song you're playing," Naniso said.

"*Manheru* — good evening. My name is Tarirai. Welcome to Tirivhu." The boy looked up and introduced himself.

"I'm Naniso. This is Shinga."

"*Vachengeti*, the Lady-Elder Baboon has disappeared. Everyone mainly calls her Lady-Elder Gudo," Tarirai reported.

"Oh. A baboon has disappeared. Is that why you are playing that song?" Naniso asked.

"To help her and us remember, yes," Tarirai replied.

"Well, if she's gone, it's not as if she'll hear it," Shinga said rudely.

"*Muchengeti*, you do know why we sing each other's songs, right?" Tarirai asked Shinga. The

76

young boy looked confused and turned from Shinga to the chameleon on his shoulder.

"Is that a trick question?" Shinga wondered out loud.

"You need to figure these things out yourself," the chameleon spoke much to Shinga's surprise.

"I think I know you!" Naniso exclaimed excitedly. "You're Rwaivhi, the chameleon!"

"The chameleon? Wait a second. We can talk to animals. Do we have magical powers too?" Shinga was amazed. He pinched Naniso to check it was all real. She cried out in pain, unimpressed.

"You have to figure these things out yourself. We can only do so much," Rwaivhi repeated bopping her golden and green head from side to side.

"This is Bao, he is a...," Tarirai began.

"Baobab tree," Shinga chipped in. "Tree of life, source of food and shelter. What are all these patterns on him?" Shinga paced around the tree. The patterns stretched from the roots right up to the top branches.

"It's as if they change to a rhythm," Naniso said joining him. They took a closer look.

"A heartbeat," they both shouted in unison before making heartbeat sounds with their voices. Tarirai joined in and started to dance joyfully. Naniso and Shinga could not resist and soon joined young Tarirai. They danced all manner of crazy moves to their heartbeat *acapella* until they collapsed with laughter on one of Bao's enormous roots.

"Tarirai, tell us again about the Lady-Elder Baboon?" Naniso asked.

"Well, everyone has been talking about it for years."

"Years!?" The twins both asked.

"Yes, the younger *sere*—that's the eight baboon children—squabbled a lot. They could not agree on anything. Each one thought they were more important than the other. One morning the eight woke up to find a huge rock left by the entrance of their home and the Lady-Elder Gudo gone. They said the sculptor had done it—*Muvezi* had turned her into stone. Later, a brave *Muchengeti* tried to get him to reverse the spell, but he also disappeared." Tarirai finished in a haunted whisper.

"But why would *Muvezi* turn someone into stone?" Shinga asked.

"That's why you are here *Muchengeti*. To help the baboons and find the sculptor," Rwaivhi said impatiently.

At this rate, it would be midnight by the time the twins figured out their mission. She had hoped they were smarter than they were showing themselves to be right now.

"You mean us? You want us to disappear like the other guy?" Shinga asked.

"Yes us," Naniso said. "This must mean you have something to learn. That's why you are here in Tirivhu."

"Err... don't forget you're here too Naniso. You must also have a lesson to learn," Shinga shot back. "Okay, I'll play along to this game. Magical powers and missing baboons."

"Don't forget a mysterious rock and *Muvezi* too. We need clues," Naniso said.

"Hmmm when we were dancing, I noticed that there was a part of Bao's magical pattern that was not changing in time with the beat." Shinga got up to show the others.

"Here it is. See," Shinga pointed at the bit of Bao's trunk that did not glow as brightly as the rest. In fact, the pattern was barely visible. They all stared hard at the fading pattern, as if willing it to get brighter.

"Tarirai please can you play the song you were playing when we got here? Music and magic always work together," Naniso asked.

"Okay," Tarirai grabbed his *mbira* excitedly. He began to play.

"Nothing's happening," Shinga said adjusting his glasses to look at the bark more closely. He wasn't sure what to expect. "Try playing louder," he suggested.

Tarirai did as he was told and plucked at the *mbira* keys harder, but nothing happened. As Tarirai continued to play, Naniso and Shinga found themselves humming along and then as though someone had counted them in, *1-2-3*, they started to sing:

Kachembere kegudo
(the old lady baboon)
Kanevana vasere
(she had eight children)
Kaifamba kachikwira mugomo
(she walked up the mountain)
Kaifamba mangwanani
(she walked in the morning)
Kachitsvaga zvekudya
(looking for something to eat)
Kanakoguta unonzwa koti yuwi yuwi
(when she was full you heard her say
'yuwi yuwi')
Kwenyu Kwenyu
(she scratches and scratches)
Kachikwira mugomo
(climbing up the mountain)
Kaifamba mangwanani
(she walked in the morning)
Kachitsvaga zvekudya
(looking for something to eat)

"Wowza! Look at this," Shinga exclaimed. Bao was glowing. To their wonder, his gentle yet enchanting glow covered the savannah plain.

"Those must be the clues! I've never seen the bark do that," Tarirai gasped.

Bao's bark showed bright images of a mountain trail, a cave and a fruit tree. The children stood astonished by the discovery. Rwaivhi quickly scurried to the spot where the magical pattern on Bao's trunk had disappeared.

"Look," she nodded. The children could now clearly see an image of a baboon.

"What do we do? Do we have to touch it or something?" Shinga asked the others.

"Remember the key I gave you last time you were here. It might work," Tarirai suggested.

It took a few moments for Shinga to recall Tarirai handing him a stone the last time he imagined this place. Surely it had just been a dream, like this one? Shinga nervously looked at his clutched hand and slowly peeled his fingers open to reveal

a stone. He placed the stone on the image of the baboon and instantly an opening appeared in the tree.

"No way!" The twins echoed each other.

"I've never seen that happen either," Tarirai was giddy with excitement. "Let's go in. I can't wait to tell..." He went through the entrance without a second thought.

"Wait!" Shinga called out. "What's he doing? We don't know where that even leads to. We need a plan."

"We must follow him." Naniso was already going through the opening.

CHAPTER 10

CLUES AND PATHS

A gust of wind greeted the twins as they walked into the tree. It picked up force and speed with every step they made, as if trying to stop them from going forward. Expecting to find themselves in yet another mystical world, the twins were somewhat disappointed to find that they were still in Tirivhu. However, they had been teleported to the foot of the mountain that had seemed so far away.

They found Tarirai standing near a foot path. The ground around his feet glowed with precious stones and a beam of light cast a trail up the mountain.

"It's never safe going up the mountain. You don't know what danger awaits you. If you go

around the mountain, the path is straight and will lead you to the sculptor," a whirlwind warned Tarirai.

"This wind makes me nervous. Do you know him Tarirai? The clue on Bao showed a path up the mountain," Naniso said.

"It's just *Sekuru* Nhema," Tarirai replied.

"Ah a clue. But have you considered that it was a warning to avoid the path up the mountain? It is dangerous," Nhema slyly hinted.

"It makes sense. The clues cannot be that simple. The wind is right. It's a warning. We need to stay safe and go around the mountain," Shinga agreed.

"Good choice," Nhema responded and led the way.

"I'm not sure about this," Naniso protested but Shinga was not paying attention. He was rushing behind the whirlwind. Naniso had no choice but to follow her brother and asked Tarirai to join them. Something about that whirlwind really unsettled her.

Around the mountain they walked. The warm sun was a welcome hug compared to the cold and wet weather the twins were used to. As they continued their journey, they saw a herd of gazelles and giraffe eating leaves from an acacia tree. The smoke from a kitchen fire in the distant village was a signal to start Shinga's stomach rumbling. A village could also mean they were near the sculptor's home. The path was indeed as smooth as Nhema had promised. But just as they had started to relax a little, a river full of crocodiles came into view. It blocked their path.

The crocodiles swam excitedly in circles at the prospect of a good meal coming their way.

They snapped their teeth and opened their huge jaws ready to ambush their prey.

"*Garwe* and his family will not let you through. We must head back," Rwaivhi finally spoke. "You must work together *Vachengeti*. There is only so much we can say and do."

"So, you knew this was a dead end?" Shinga was upset at Rwaivhi.

"Yes," Rwaivhi replied. "I am sorry, but you must figure this out yourselves."

"This is so annoying," Shinga stomped off back in the direction they had come. Truth be told, he was more annoyed with himself. He knew he should have trusted Naniso and Tarirai. It was then that Shinga realised the whirlwind, Nhema had gone. He had been tricked.

"This is silly. I am ten years old. I want out of this dream. I need to wake up right now!" Shinga cried out.

"I don't think giving up is supposed to be your life lesson," Naniso nudged her brother hoping to calm him. "I know you're worried about your football trials. You have not been yourself because of the pressure. You cannot give up on your dreams just because things don't go to plan. You can do this. We can do this."

Shinga smiled at Naniso. It was true that ever since meeting the old man in the park, he was full of doubts about his talents, his friends and his family. He suddenly had a light bulb moment and perked up.

"That's it. I know what I need to learn. Bravery! We must go up the mountain. Commitment! We must finish what we started. Teamwork! We must work together. And from now on, I will listen and be positive."

These were all the opposite of the names that old man had called him. It was the key to solving the problem.

"Now, that's what I call a winner's speech," Rwaivhi said and laughed with delight.

"Okay, let's race back!" Tarirai shouted, already on his way. Accepting the challenge, the twins ran after him.

CHAPTER 11

UP THE MOUNTAIN

They were back to the start of the trail that gleamed with precious minerals and did not hesitate to follow it up. With every footstep that Tarirai made, the path lit up guiding them up the mountain. Naniso's eyes grew with excitement at the treasure chest beneath their feet.

"There you are," Nhema, the whirlwind said swirling around them with a chuckle. "I lost you. Where did you go? I see you've decided to take this route. Let me help move the tall grass out of the way." He swiftly blew the tall grass before anyone could reply.

"I don't trust him," Naniso whispered to Shinga.

"I'm not sure of him either. Let's keep an eye on him," Shinga agreed.

The twins looked at each other. It all seemed weird, yet very familiar. They loved an adventure, and it would certainly be lovely to see where this dream would take them.

"*Pamwe*," they both said as they high-fived each other in the way they always did when they were about to work together. Then they continued to follow the golden trail behind Tarirai.

Suddenly there were raised voices. Without saying a word to each other, the trio and Rwaivhi followed the sounds off the path and into tall grass that dwarfed them. They came across a cave. It was dark and eerie. Shinga could make out eight baboons that were in a very heated argument. Next to the baboons was a large rock that they seemed to be guarding.

"Hello?" Shinga said hesitantly.

"Ah *Vachengeti*," the baboons said, not at all surprised to see them.

"Why are you arguing?" Shinga asked.

That question alone set the baboons quarrelling again. Their barks and grunts were deafening. Shinga, Naniso and Tarirai stood shocked, unsure of what to do. Out of the blue, Rwaivhi flicked her long tongue up at each baboon's angry face. Eight accurate and slimy flicks. Urgh! It caught the baboons by surprise and shushed them.

With calm restored, it turned out the group blamed each other for the Lady Elder Gudo's disappearance. They squabbled about everything. From whose turn it was to go foraging to why they were sitting next to each other. The constant fighting clearly left them tired, hungry and irritable. They all agreed on one thing though — how delicious the mango that grew on the tree at the top of the mountain would be. That used to be Lady Elder Gudo's favourite treat.

Once, they said, a boy about the twins' age, a *Muchengeti*, gave them a message. He had said the baboons needed to work together and take the rock to the top of the mountain. Only there the sculptor could free the Lady Elder Gudo. It had only taken a few moments of them all working together before they had given up. The boy had tried his best to encourage them to act as a team, but it was no use.

"Why did you give up?" Naniso asked.

"You thought it would take too long to get the stone up the mountain," said one baboon pointing to another.

"Yes, yes," the others barked in agreement.

"It's not that. What if it had rolled all the way down to the bottom of the mountain and heaven forbid, cracked into a million tiny pieces," the accused baboon replied. "Where would that leave Lady Elder Gudo?"

"Probably blowing in the wind," said another baboon, "and then the sculptor would come and turn us into stone instead!"

Soon the arguing started again.

Naniso, Shinga and Tarirai huddled.

"It's obvious," Shinga said, "we need to take the rock to the mango tree. That was the other image on Bao's bark."

96

"They seem a bit discombobulated. We need to help them. They can't do this themselves," Naniso said.

"I agree. Let's see... the last *Muchengeti* left a message to say the rock needs to go to the top of the mountain. That is what we'll do," Shinga stated.

Tarirai and Naniso nodded in agreement. Shinga turned to address the eight baboons, when suddenly the cave was clouded with blinding dust.

"No one is going up the mountain with that rock," Nhema roared.

"It's the obvious thing to do. We can help them," Shinga said to the whirlwind.

"No one!" Nhema's voice rumbled and echoed across the mountains. Ignoring Nhema. Shinga pleaded with the baboons.

"Everyone quick, don't argue. Please, please don't argue. We must move the rock. We are taking it to the top of the mountain."

"We can't go there. We'll be turned to stone." The eight baboons moved backwards further into the cave.

"Listen, what does a sculptor do? He brings out the beauty of the stone. I don't believe that he turned Lady Elder into this. It doesn't make sense. Besides when we get there, there will be the sweetest mangos for us all."

The baboons made their own huddle. There was a lot of grunting—good grunting. Defying Nhema's orders the eight turned the rock onto its side and began to roll it up the mountain. The twins and Tarirai helped them. There was excitement and a feeling of togetherness. Shinga shouted words of encouragement, just like he had heard Coach do at practice.

Rwaivhi jumped from one baboon's back to the other, encouraging them along. At times, the team lost their footing, tripping over undergrowth and lost a bit of distance. Other times, someone got tired, but they kept moving and helped each other along. They had somewhere to be, so they all buckled up and continued.

Suddenly, a dark heavy cloud descended on them making it difficult to see the way. Then, climbers furiously sprouted from the ground, knitting together around the group and enclosing them into a cage. They were trapped.

"Nhema! Leave them alone!" Rwaivhi shouted.

"He will fail!" Nhema shouted back.

"Hey, I'm right here! I won't fail!" Shinga was more determined than ever because it was all down to him now. He had heard Nhema's voice before because the menace that laced it was familiar. He could feel a knot take hold in his stomach. Everyone depended on him. He had to stay focused so he called to the others to keep moving forward, hoping the climbers would snap with force. All of them—Naniso, Tarirai, Rwaivhi and the baboons—pushed the rock against the cage until the climbers buckled.

Tarirai was the first to leap ahead. "The ground is covered with these pesky climbers trying to grab our legs. Mind where you step!"

"We must move faster," Shinga instructed. Secretly he prayed that no one would spoil things and start an argument. There was no room for doubt now. They were almost there.

Naniso started to hum the song '*Kachembere kegudo*' and they all joined in. It was fuel for the uphill climb and ointment for their aching muscles.

Suddenly Rwaivhi shouted, "Duck!"

A vulture swooped angrily down towards them narrowly missing their heads. Nhema, who had been frozen in shock at how the group had broken free from his cage, joined the vulture and tried to push the group back. Boulders came crashing down from the sky, blocking Shinga and his friends again.

An evil laugh filled the air. Nhema spoke in a voice that made Shinga shudder. "You will fail because you are rough, negative. You lack commitment. You are not a team player."

Wasn't it the voice of the old man from the park? The old man who would not give him his football back and had called him all sorts of names?

"I knew this wind was fishy," Naniso whispered to Shinga. "Let me distract him and you get the baboons and the rock to the top somehow."

"I think it's me he's after Naniso, so you need to lead the team now. Tarirai, work your magic and move those boulders so everyone can get through to the other side."

"I will," Tarirai said confidently.

"Use your footsteps to find the golden path and the climbers won't get you," Shinga added.

"What are you going to do?" Naniso sounded worried.

"If I look like I've given up, Nhema will think it's over and leave you all alone. He expects me to fail so I will hang back and pretend to quit."

"Rwaivhi wants to come with you," Tarirai said and placed the chameleon on Shinga's shoulder.

"Be careful," Naniso warned.

"You too," her twin replied.

CHAPTER 12

THE SCULPTOR

Shinga fell back behind the others dragging his feet. Nhema kept close to him. The haunting murmur of the wind whistled through the trees. Nhema mocked Shinga relentlessly for suddenly abandoning his team. Each step was echoed with Nhema's name-calling. It took all the will Shinga had to not respond. He kept the pretence as this kept Nhema focused solely on him.

Shinga stole glances up the mountain. He saw Tarirai using his magical powers to move the boulders out of the way, and it looked super cool. Naniso, like a commander, guided the team to the other side. They were advancing slowly but stealthily so as not to rouse Nhema's attention. Shinga was momentarily distracted by the thought of the mangos that awaited them. Always one to be distracted by food, Shinga tripped as a result and a climber wrapped around his ankles. He could not move forward.

"Now Bao will see that I was right after all," Nhema swirled around Shinga. "You will never reveal the secret message in that stone."

"But the rock has revealed its secret already," Shinga told Nhema.

"No! *Muvezi* has not attended to it. It cannot be. How?" Nhema could not believe his ears. He circled faster around Shinga to intimidate him.

"Stop it! Why are you like this?" Shinga asked.

"Well, what were you expecting to see. A superhero?" Nhema scoffed.

It became clear to Shinga that the bedtime stories Ruzivo told were adventures in Tirivhu. The mountain, the cave and the mango tree were in his stories. Ruzivo was the *Muchengeti* the baboons spoke about.

"You're definitely not the hero Ruzivo talks so fondly about. What happened to you? You guided *Mukoma* Ruzivo on amazing adventures and protected and warned Tirivhu of 'The Lie'. Have you forgotten who you are *Sekuru Nhemadzinoparira?* That's your full name, right?" Shinga continued, "I don't know what happened to *Mukoma* Ruzivo, but I know I'm also here to finish this mission for him."

"Ruzivo...," Nhema's voice softened into a whisper. He slowly shape-shifted into his human form. His eyes glistened with tears.

Before Shinga, stood the old man from the park. Everything was still. The stillness reminded Shinga of the time between the end of worship and start of a sermon at church. A change or transformation. The old man, Nhema, nodded at Shinga then to Rwaivhi, swept up in a breeze and vanished.

"Look Shinga! The climbers have gone!" shouted Rwaivhi, pointing at Shinga's feet.

It was time to catch up with the others. Shinga immediately jumped up. As they walked, each step Shinga made lit the jewelled pathway.

"Look at how rich the land we walk on is, Rwaivhi. I don't even know the names of all these precious stones."

Finally at the top of the mountain, Shinga was reunited with Naniso, Tarirai and the eight baboons. His eyes could not believe what was before them. There stretched across the top of the mountain range, as far as one could see, were all manner of sculptures rising from the ground. They were made from different types of stone like serpentine, spring stone, leopard rock and verdite, and were perfectly formed, smooth and shiny. Each sculpture represented a family of all the animal species in Tirivhu. The rock they had pushed up the mountain blended perfectly with the sculptures despite its roughness and ragged edges.

"It's about family, but I don't see a sculpture of baboons," Naniso said.

"It's time to find out what happened to Lady Elder Gudo," Shinga said pacing round the rock they had pushed up. The largest of the eight baboons offered Shinga a juicy mango to help solve this mystery. As they all walked slowly around the rock, the ground where the mango tree stood started to shake. Tarirai and Rwaivhi walked towards the tree and were engulfed in its golden light as it transformed into a huge baobab tree. It was Bao. His bark was even more majestic than they had seen before. The patterns showed all animals of the earth, sea and sky.

"The tree of life," the twins both gasped.

"*Chenga ose manhanga hapana risina mhodzi*," Bao was filled with delight. "Tell us the stone's message Muchengeti," Bao encouraged Shinga.

Shinga paused and thought for a while. "Family, togetherness and connection. *Ukama* like *Amai*'s sculpture from *Mukoma* Ruzivo. Today I learnt how important a family is. Like this earth, our family expands over borders, cultures and friendships." Shinga turned to smile at the baboons and then looked at Naniso adding, "It's just like us and *Mukoma* Ruzivo." He pointed at the rock and continued, "This is the baboon family sculpture. I can see Lady Elder and the eight baboon children. Here is The Lady Elder acting as the frame and..."

"...That's me," the largest grey baboon pointed to a piece of the rock.

"That's me," another baboon pointed. In turn they all identified themselves on parts of the rock.

"We have the outline of the sculpture. I will need to get rid of the rock that is not part of it. I must remove the rough texture with a hammer, then smooth the surfaces. The sculptors I've seen use a grinder and a chisel. You'll all have to help." Shinga was speaking like an expert, and they all nodded.

"We need to wash and sand the sculpture. We'll need to polish it, apply wax and buff with a cloth. Then we'll need to heat it so an adult would have to help us."

"You are *Muvezi*, Shinga. Did you hear what you just said?" Naniso exclaimed.

"Yes indeed, you are," Bao said with pride. "But it will take you a long time to do all that work."

"I guess if you really want something, you have to go for it. You have to have commitment and accept help," Shinga responded.

"Then let me, Bao of Tirivhu, help you," Bao offered.

With those words a blinding golden light shone from his trunk onto the rock. The rock spun round and round and floated upwards. As it spun, a golden chisel appeared, removing chunks of excess stone. Then a magical chalk drew a precise outline of the baboon family exactly as Shinga had pointed out. Once the crayon was done a golden chisel carefully added texture to the work. Small stone chips and dust blew away in the wind revealing a tall brown-orange sculpture of Lady Elder Gudo and the eight baboon children. Finally, eight pieces of sandpaper polished the sculpture giving it a beautiful shine. It was breathtaking.

"This is me," a frail old voice said. Next to the sculpture stood an old grey baboon. She looked fragile yet regal. It was Lady Elder Gudo.

"You have done well *Vachengeti*. My family now understand that they are a team. How beautiful we look. Thank you," Lady Elder Gudo said as the baboon children rushed with excitement to greet her.

"Thank you," Tarirai echoed. "You see it could have been easy to give up on the baboons. But you brought out their most precious jewel, their strength as a family." With that, he settled on one of Bao's roots to play a *mbira* that had mysteriously appeared from nowhere.

CHAPTER 13

SHINGA MAKES AMENDS

It only took a nod and smile from Bao and the twins instantly found themselves out of Tirivhu and back in the park. A lady pushing a jolly toddler in a stroller smiled at them. Their ice-cream was melting. They looked at each other questioningly. Had they both really been on a mystical adventure?

"Tirivhu," Naniso said hoping the word made sense to Shinga

"Tirivhu," Shinga smiled, licking ice cream off his fingers.

"Hey you two! Hurry up! Let's play ball," Ruzivo called out. He was counting kick-ups. Shinga got up and ran to hug Ruzivo almost knocking him to the ground. He wanted to fix

things and hoped it was not too late. Ruzivo chuckled warmly hugging him back. This was certainly unexpected.

"I'm sorry *Mukoma*," Shinga said.

Ruzivo patted him on the shoulder, a gesture acknowledging the apology. "It's alright little man. You've had a lot to deal with in the past few weeks."

"But can you help me? I know you played in one of the biggest football teams in Zim. You were a fantastic striker. I'm sorry about your injury. You know what I need to do. Will you help me train? I'm afraid Coach may have lost his confidence in me." Shinga's sentences ran one into the other.

"Firstly, my knee injury wasn't your fault. Secondly, of course, I'll help you. But I won't make it easy just because I am your brother." Ruzivo tried to look stern.

"I have something else to tell you," Shinga lowered his voice.

"Yes Shinga?" Ruzivo was curious.

"The baboons found the mango tree and the Lady Elder."

Ruzivo gave a hearty laugh. His eyes sparkled as he waggled his eyebrow comically. "And I thought you didn't pay attention to my silly made-up stories. Looks like it's your turn to tell me a bedtime story."

"Please may you both help me fix *Amai*'s sculpture. I must apologise to her. Naniso, I will ask *Baba* to give you your phone back. It's not fair for you to be punished for my mistake," Shinga said apologetically.

Ruzivo and Naniso gave him a group hug of assurance.

"Hey Shinga. Your friends Sanjay and Mason are here," Naniso pointed out.

Shinga's friends joined them full of excitement. They recounted how Ruzivo had helped them earlier that afternoon at Startbots to build a baboon out of Lego. The 'sculpture' could even dance with the help of some coding.

"It was awesome," Mason kept repeating.

"C'mon, we worked together. You helped me build and code it," smiled Ruzivo.

"Ruzivo you need to teach us that song you sang for the Lego baboon to dance to," Sanjay requested.

"*Kachembere kegudo*?" The twins said at the same time.

Gogo Zana drank from a cup of tea as she keenly watched her brother. Nhema was looking at his face in a mirror. He turned his head left to right, up and down and noticed how the once deep wrinkles had smoothed out a little. He had been staring at that mirror for a while now. Bao who had his eyes closed was also patiently waiting for Nhema to break the silence.

The mention of Ruzivo would bring tears into Nhema's eyes. Zana and Bao waited for his cue. A flock of violet-eared waxbill or *chisiisii*, foraged on the ground nearby. In the distance, a pack of wild dogs sprinted across the savannah plain.

"Ruzivo. He remembers me. He does not blame me," Nhema finally spoke.

"He has not forgotten you," Bao agreed.

"But how?" Nhema touched his face examining each wrinkle.

"The embers keep burning. They never go cold. The flame is alive," Bao said with joy.

"Ruzivo kept everything that was good about you, shared it with Shinga and helped save the day," Zana explained.

"We must celebrate this and how young Tarirai made such a great companion," Bao beamed.

Nhema's earlier vulnerability was now replaced by an evil smirk.

"This has all been intriguing but I'm not convinced. The boy was lucky. These people cannot be trusted seeing as they left Tirivhu. We can have all the power we need with the treasure here. Imagine how powerful we would be," Nhema ranted.

Zana sighed with disappointment. She watered the black velvet flower that now had streaks of yellow. What was it going to take to convince her brother that the heritage treasure was worth protecting and sharing with its rightful heirs within and outside Tirivhu? Nhema was looking at his face again in the mirror. He was truly a complicated mix of hero and villain.

"You need to let go of your anger *Nhemadzinoparira* and have some trust," Bao advised. "Remember — *Chenga ose manhanga hapana risina mhodzi* — Take care of all the pumpkins because there is none without seed. We all have a purpose. We are all important."

...To be continued...

GLOSSARY

Amai	mother
Ambuya	grandmother
Baba	father
Babamukuru	father's older brother (*older father*)
Chisiisii	violet-eared waxbill
Dhuku	headwrap
Gara pasi	sit down
Garwe	crocodile
Gogo	granny
Gudo	baboon
Hanzvadzi	sister (*if a brother is speaking*), brother (*if a sister is speaking*)
Hongu	yes
Ini	me/I
Iwe	you
Kachembere keGudo	an old female baboon
Makadi	how are you

Mangwanani	good morning
Manheru	good evening
Masikati	good afternoon
Mazvita	thank you
Mbira	thumb piano
Muchengeti	guardian
Mukoma	older brother/sister
Munin'ina	young brother by age (*if older brother speaking*) younger sister by age (*if older sister speaking*)
Muriwo	green vegetables
Muvezi	sculptor
Naniso	something spectacular, marvelous
Nhema	lies
Nhemadzino-parira	lies are destructive
Pamwe	together
Roora	a traditional marriage process by which one gets a wife in the Shona custom

Ruzivo	wisdom
Sadza	Sadza is the traditional food of Zimbabwe. It is a stiff porridge made of maizemeal and is often served with meat stew and vegetables. Across Africa it is known by various names e.g fufu, ugali, nshima
Sekuru	grandfather
Sere	eight
Shinga	to be brave
Siya	leave it/them
Tarirai	to look after
Tete	father's sister, a paternal aunt
Tirivhu	we are earth
Tsika	manners
Tsumo	proverbs
Ubuntu	showing goodwill/humanity towards others. The word comes from the Xhosa and Zulu languages and is often described as "I am what I am because of who we all are."

Ukama	how we are related to each other
Vachengeti	guardians
Yako	yours
Zana	a hundred
Zvakwana	enough
Zvose	everything

Rina manyanga hariputirwe mumushunje—that which has horns cannot be hidden in a bundle of grass. This proverb means that no matter how hard you may try to hide something wrong it will always come to light.

Chenga ose manhanga hapana risina mhodzi—take care of all the pumpkins, there is none without seed. This is a proverb that means we should treat everyone equally because we are all important.

Kachembere kegudo—this is a fun folk song that children in Zimbabwe and those in the diaspora sing and dance to during play. You can listen to a version of it at *www.nanisoshinga.com*

Shona Lyrics

Kachembere kegudo

Kanevana vasere

Kaifamba kachikwira mugomo

Kaifamba mangwanani

Kachitsvaga zvekudya

Kanakoguta unonzwa koti yuwi yuwi

Kwenyu Kwenyu

Kachikwira mugomo

Kaifamba mangwanani

Kachitsvaga zvekudya

English Translation

The old lady baboon

She had eight children

She walked up the mountain

She walked in the morning

Looking for something to eat

When she was full you heard her say 'yuwi yuwi'

She scratches and scratches

As she climbed up the mountain

She walked in the morning

Looking for something to eat

OTHER BOOKS
IN THE NANISO & SHINGA SERIES

The Mysterious Melody
ISBN: 978-1-9161217-06

OTHER BOOKS BY SP K-MUSHAMBI

Tarirai's Choice
ISBN: 978-1-9161217-20

To find out more about the twins and their friends go to
www.nanisoshinga.com.

NanisoCreate

NanisoCreate is guided by the motto **'Imagine it. Create it. Inspire.'** Our objective is to use storytelling, education and events in a fun and imaginative way.

We believe that literature and media that reflect our stories, our experiences and our images are essential for inspiring self-esteem and a sense of belonging. Diverse representation is not just a gateway to other worlds and cultures, but also brings hope, comfort and enable children to have empathy and respect for others.

Find out more at *www.nanisocreate.com*,
or search for *@NanisoCreate*.

ABOUT THE AUTHOR

SP K-Mushambi is happiest when she is creating. It could be writing a song, baking a yummy cake or inventing her own version of the latest dance craze (which according to reliable sources means she is doing it all wrong). She enjoys getting to know different cultures and how they are related to her own heritage.

Born in England and raised in Zimbabwe, she has had a career in banking and corporate treasury which spans over twenty years. She lives in Berkshire with her husband and their two daughters.